THE FOG

WORDS BY KYO MACLEAR
PICTURES BY KENARD PAK

TUNDRA BOOKS

Far north, on a wild sea, was an island covered with ice.

#668
WHISTLING
GREAT-EARED
FEMALE

#676 GREATER YELLOW LEGS

#677
LESSER
YELLOW LEGS

#678
ROADRUNNER

#679 PURPLE MARTIN

SHOVEL

#669
HAIRY
ORANGE-
CROWNED
MALE
(JUVENILE)

BOOKS

#670
APPER BESPECTACLED
BOOKLOVER

#674
SWIFT
RED-CAPPED
PITCHER

People came from around the world to visit this special place.

Most of the birds living on the island paid little
attention to these visitors. But there was one bird,
a small yellow warbler, who did pay attention.

Warble was a devoted human watcher.

There was always a new human for him to watch.
Nothing else Warble did made him happier.

#671 BEHATTED
BIBLIOPHILIC
FEMALE

#672 BALD-HEADED
GLITZY MALE

But one spring day, something
happened to interrupt his happiness.

That day, a warm fog rolled in from the sea. All morning long,
it wisped and swirled, climbing hills and spilling into valleys.

By lunchtime, the brightness of morning had faded to a silvery blue.
By dinnertime, the fog had turned everything ghostly.

For days, Warble sat high in his tree and waited for a strong gust of wind to come lift the fog. He waited and waited.

Being a handy warbler,
he tried to chase it away.

But, no matter what he did, the fog came back.
Warble invited his neighbors over to discuss the situation.

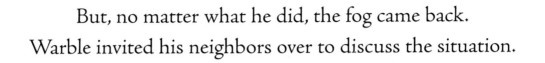

IT'S JUST A LITTLE FOG.
I WOULDN'T EVEN CALL IT FOG.
MIST, MAYBE. ETHER, PERHAPS. FOG, NO.

THE FOG HAS COME.
SOMETIMES THESE THINGS HAPPEN.
LET US BE HUMBLE AND ACCEPT IT.

I LIKE WHAT IT DOES TO MY FEATHERS.

Only the ducks seemed to care.

The next morning, a new sign appeared.

WELCOME
TO
FOG LAND

The re-naming of the island had a curious effect.
Many of the birds began to forget that
there was ever a time before the fog.

But Warble did not forget.
And he had started to notice other changes too.

HERE'S LOOKING AT YOU, KID.

He went to tell the others what he
had seen but they were too busy.

HOW TO BRIGHTEN YOUR HOME
WITH 1000 WATT NEST LIGHTS

Even the ducks had moved on
and didn't want to talk about it.

The fog continued to spread.

Warble still waited in his tree,
hoping to spot a human,
but there were no more sightings.

So he put away his books and tried his best to
ignore the fog. Until even *he* began to wonder
if things had ever been any different.

FOGGY
MOUNTAIN
BOYS

But then, one foggy morning,
Warble spotted a colorful speck in the distance.

Peering closely, he saw a dark-haired human
ghosting through the meadow. It was a rare female species
and she was singing a song.

#673 RED-HOODED SPECTACLED
FEMALE (JUVENILE)

She looked a bit lost.

Happy to see a human again,
Warble offered her insects to eat.

She liked them.

The human, in return, offered Warble gifts
and showed him how to fold intricate paper things.

And there they stayed, eating insects and folding paper
and speaking in every way except with words.

Until Warble made a surprising discovery . . .

The human also saw the fog.

Warble asked the human if she thought there
were others who saw the fog too. She was unsure.
How could they find out?

That's when she had an idea. She opened her backpack
and set to work. The human made a paper boat
and floated it out to sea.

DO YOU SEE
THE FOG?

They waited for a reply but none arrived.

WORMS

So they launched more boats. And, again, they waited.

Finally, they had an answer.

It was a note from a walrus
in eastern Canada.

Another note came from
a musk ox in Norway.

Another came from
some cats in England.

Notes arrived from around the world.

With each one, the fog began to lift a little.
And the wind began to blow again until the world grew
a little less ghostly and it became easier to notice things.

Big things.

And tiny things.

And soft
feathery things.

Shiny red things.

And slowly, slowly, the beautiful island brightened,
and Warble and the human found time to rest under the stars,
which they could now see.

The moon drifted in the sky. And they began to sing.
They sang to each other and to the moon and
because they were happy to be together,
sharing the clear night view.

FOR NAOMI K. AND NAOMI B.W.
WITH THANKS TO KEN, TARA AND SCOTT
(NICEST AND BRIGHTEST OF HUMANS)
— K.M.

TO BEN AND LEEANNA
— K.P.

TEXT COPYRIGHT © 2017 BY KYO MACLEAR
ILLUSTRATIONS COPYRIGHT © 2017 BY KENARD PAK

Tundra Books, a division of Random House of Canada Limited, a Penguin Random House Company

LIBRARY AND ARCHIVES CANADA CATALOGUING IN PUBLICATION

Maclear, Kyo, 1970-, author
The fog / Kyo Maclear ; illustrated by Kenard Pak.
Issued in print and electronic formats.
ISBN 978-1-77049-492-3 (hardback).—ISBN 978-1-77049-493-0 (epub)
1. Pak, Kenard, illustrator 11. Title.

PS8625.L435F64 2017   jC813'.6   C2016-900974-2   C2016-900975-0

Published simultaneously in the United States of America by Tundra Books of Northern New York,
a division of Random House of Canada Limited, a Penguin Random House Company

LIBRARY OF CONGRESS CONTROL NUMBER: 2016933019

Edited by Tara Walker, a Brown-Crested Meddler
The artist used pencil, watercolor and digital work to make the illustrations in this book.
The text was set in Adobe Jenson. Handlettering by Kenard Pak.
Printed and bound in China

www.penguinrandomhouse.ca

1 2 3 4 5   21 20 19 18 17

Penguin
Random
House
TUNDRA BOOKS

#659 WHOOPING BUFF-CHESTED MALE (JUVENILE)

#661 WHITE-HATTED HERMIT

#667 SILVER-CRESTED CLAPPER (ELDER)

PILLBOX

#660 MASKED BOHEMIAN WEAVER

#664 AMERICAN BUSHY-BROWED SURF-HEAD

#662 VELVET-COATED SINGER

#666 SOLITARY KNITTER

HEADPHONES

#663 SPOTTED AUDIOPHILIC FEMALE (JUVENILE)

#665 ROBIN (JUVENILE)